Natalie Jean and The HAINTS' PARADE

by Kersten Hamilton
pictures by Susan Harrison

Tyndale House Publishers
Wheaton, Illinois

To Megan
My Inspiration

Library of Congress Cataloging-in-Publication Data

Hamilton, K. R. (Kersten R.)
Natalie Jean and the haints' parade / by Kersten Hamilton ; pictures by Susan Harrison.
p. cm. — (Natalie Jean adventures ; bk. 4)
Summary: Natalie Jean asks Jesus to help her overcome her fear of those strange ghostly noises she hears everywhere.
ISBN 0-8423-4622-8 (pbk.)
[1. Courage — Fiction. 2. Christian life — Fiction.] I. Harrison, Susan, ill. II. Title. III. Series: Hamilton, K. R. (Kersten R.). Natalie Jean adventures ; bk. 4.
PZ7.H1824Nav 1991 90-72052
[E] — dc20

Book development by March Media, Inc., Brentwood, Tennessee

Printed in the United States of America

98 97 96 95 94 93 92 91
9 8 7 6 5 4 3 2 1

CONTENTS

Chapter 1

Grand-mother Wander

“I am glad you came to walk home
with me, Samson,” said Natalie Jean.
“Meow,” said Samson.
The wind whispered in the dry cornstalks
beside the road.
Natalie thought it sounded scary.

"Do not worry, Samson," Natalie said.

She looked around. "I will take care of you."

Samson rubbed against her leg.

"Buster Biddle put a dead mouse in my lunch pail," Natalie said.

"Meow?" said Samson.

"Of course, I saved it for you," said Natalie.

On the road ahead, Natalie saw a tiny old woman.

"Good afternoon, Grandmother Wander," Natalie said.

"Good afternoon, Natalie. Samson is looking very handsome today."

Grandmother Wander was clipping here and snipping there and dropping roses in a basket.

"These roses will be gone soon," she said.

She tucked a rose in Natalie's hair.

"It makes me sad to say good-by to them until spring."

Brown leaves blew around their feet.

"Oh, my," said Grandmother Wander.

"The wind is chilly today!"

"Samson thinks the wind is scary," said Natalie.

"He does?" Grandmother Wander said.

She put her hands on her hips.

She looked at Samson.

"My, my," she said and shook her head.

"I guess everybody is afraid sometimes."

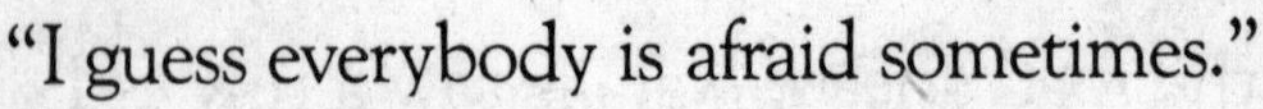

"Are you afraid sometimes?" Natalie asked.

"Yes, I am," Grandmother Wander laughed.

"When I am afraid, I talk to the Lord Jesus. I think about his angels watching over me. That helps me be brave."

Natalie looked in the cornfield.
She looked in the tree.
But she did not see any angels.
"Are you sure there are angels?"
Natalie asked.
"I read it in my Bible, child," said
Grandmother Wander. "It must be true."

"Meow," said Samson.
He looked at the lunch pail.
"You are right, Samson," said Natalie Jean.
"We must hurry home. Good-by,
Grandmother Wander."
Natalie ran down the road.
Samson ran too.

Natalie's sister Tessa was waiting by the gate.

"Will you come to my party in the coach house?" Tessa asked. "We will have tea and cake."

"Yes," said Natalie. "I am very hungry. I did not eat my lunch."

"Why not?" asked Tessa. She took Natalie's lunch pail.

"Buster Biddle put a dead mouse in it," Natalie said.

"Eeeeeeek," said Tessa.

She dropped the pail.

As Natalie picked up the pail, a boy jumped over the fence.

He ran right into Natalie.

Natalie sat down in the dust.

The boy sat down, too.

He looked surprised.

"Buster Biddle!" said Natalie Jean.

"What are you doing?"

Chapter 2

Buster Biddle

Buster Biddle wiped dust off his cowboy boots.
He slapped dust off his overalls.
"Better run home," he said. "I just heard a tommy-knocker, knocking in the woods."

"What is a tommy-knocker?" Tessa asked.

"A haint," said Buster Biddle.

He looked over his shoulder.

"What is a haint?" said Tessa.

"Things that moan and things that groan," said Buster Biddle. "Things that go bump behind you. And when a tommy-knocker knocks, the other haints come out. They have a haints' parade!"

"You cannot scare me, Buster Biddle,"
Natalie said. "I do not believe in haints.
And everybody knows a tommy-knocker
is just a woodpecker."
Buster Biddle's ears turned red.

"Come on, Tessa," Natalie said.
She tossed her braids.
"There will be a haints' parade,"
Buster Biddle called after them.
"Just you wait and see."

Natalie and Tessa walked to the coach house.

"The party is upstairs," said Tessa.

The corners in the coach house were dark and full of lumps.

Natalie tried not to look at them.

She climbed the stairs and looked straight ahead.

"Do you get the shivers in the coach house, Samson?" Natalie whispered.

"Meow," said Samson.

"Me, too," said Natalie.

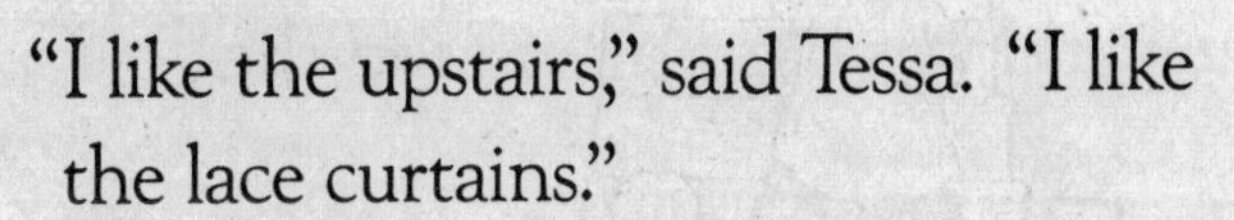

“I like the upstairs,” said Tessa. “I like the lace curtains.”
Tessa spread a red and white blanket on the floor.
A little cake was sitting on a trunk.
The teapot and teacups were on the trunk, too. It looked very pretty.

But the wind was blowing around the roof.

"Ooooooo," it said.

Natalie tried not to listen.

"You sit here," Tessa said.

Natalie sat beside Tessa's doll Lucinda.

"How are you today, Lucinda?" she asked.

Lucinda did not say anything.

Tessa poured tea into Natalie's cup.

She put in three lumps of sugar.

She started to put a piece of cake on Natalie's plate.

But she stopped.

"Look!" she said, and pointed to the white lace curtain.
It was moving back and forth, back and forth.
"There is a haint behind the curtain," Tessa whispered.
"There are no such things as haints," said Natalie Jean. "Come on, Samson."
Natalie crept close to the window.
"No, Natty, no," Tessa said. "The haint will get you!"
She covered her eyes.

Chapter 3

The Haints' Parade

Natalie grabbed the curtain.
She pulled it back.
“There is nothing here,” said Natalie Jean.
“It was only the wind.”

Tessa peeked through her fingers
to make sure.
"I am glad you are brave, Natty," she said.
She put some cake on Natalie's plate.
"Meow?" said Samson.
"Yes, Samson," said Natalie. "You may have
the dead mouse for tea."
"I want to see the dead mouse," said Tessa.

Natalie took the cover off her lunch pail.
Tessa leaned over it.
"Poor little mouse," she said.
Suddenly the mouse jumped up.
It jumped to the top of the pail.
It jumped to the top of Tessa's head.
"EEEEEEEEEEEEKKKK," screamed Tessa.
"This mouse is not dead!"

Tessa shook her head.
The mouse fell off.
It landed on the cake.
Samson jumped after it.
He landed on the cake, too.
But the mouse was too fast.
It ran behind the trunk and got away.
"That was mean, Natalie!" said Tessa.

"I thought the mouse was dead," said Natalie. "It must have been sleeping."

"I do not want to have a party anymore," said Tessa. "The cake is smashed. And the mouse might come back." She picked up her red and white blanket. She picked up Lucinda, too.

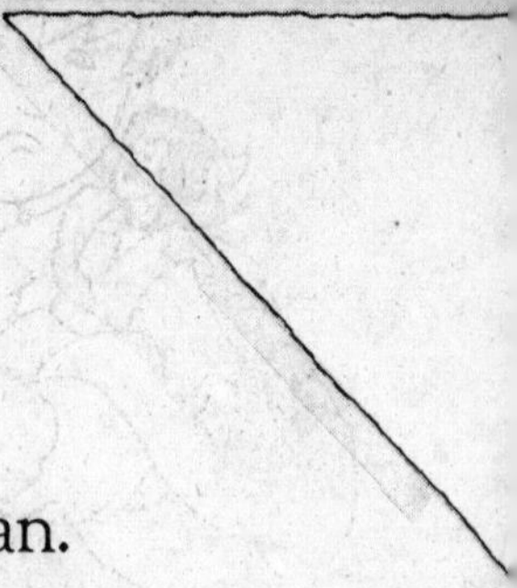

Thump, bump!
"What was that?" said Natalie Jean.
She looked down the stairs.
"Maybe it is the mouse," Tessa said.
"You are brave, Natty. You go down first.
I will come behind you."
Natalie Jean started down the stairs.
Tessa followed her.
Thump, bump!

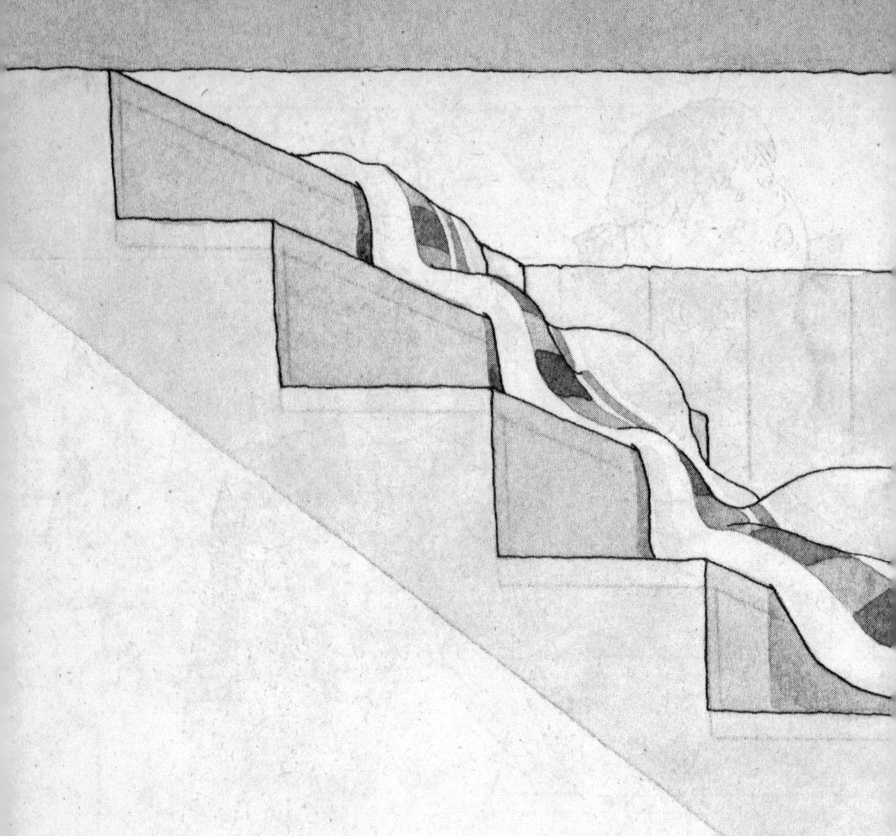

Natalie looked into the corners.
They were very dark and very lumpy.
And one of the lumps looked different.
"Go back up, Tessa," Natalie said.
"I will not," said Tessa. "The mouse is
up there. You go down."
"No," said Natalie. "There is a Thing down
there. A Thing that thumps and bumps."

"It is the haints' parade," said Tessa, "just like Buster Biddle said!"

Tessa sat down on the stairs.

She put the red and white blanket over her head.

"What are you doing?" Natalie asked.
"Hiding," said Tessa.
"But I can see you," said Natalie. "The Thing can see you, too."
"Yes," said Tessa. "But I cannot see it. And that makes me feel better."

Chapter 4

Down the Stairs

Thump, scrape!
Natalie had the shivers from her toes
to her nose.
She did not want to go down the stairs.

She wished she had a blanket to hide under.
She put her hands in her pockets and tried to look small.
Grandmother Wander's rose tickled her ear.
Natalie thought about Grandmother Wander.
She thought about Jesus and his big, strong angels.

"Jesus," Natalie whispered very quietly.

"I do not believe in haints. But I do believe in you."

"Jesus' angels are watching over me," Natalie said in a very loud voice. "And we are coming down the stairs now. ALL of us."

Tessa took the blanket off her head.

Natalie went down one step, and then another.

“Hurry, Tessa,” Natalie said.
She tried not to look at the Thing in the corner.
Just as Tessa reached the bottom, something went scrape.
The Thing was moving!
Shuffle, thump.
It came closer.
Tessa hid behind Natalie.
“Do not worry, Tessa,” Natalie said.
“Jesus is taking care of us.”

But she still felt shivery.
All at once the mouse ran down the stairs.
Samson ran after it.
The mouse scurried to the dark corner.

It ran under the Thing.
The Thing said, "Whoop! Whooooop!"
It jumped up and began to dance.
Natalie could see its feet.
They were wearing cowboy boots.
"Buster Biddle!" Natalie said. "What are you doing under that dust cover!"
Buster Biddle did not answer.
He threw the dust cover in the air.

He stomped and jumped and spun around.

"The mouse went up my pants leg," he said.

Buster Biddle and his mouse ran out the door.

Samson ran after them.

"I wish I were brave like you, Natty," Tessa said. "I was very afraid."

"Everyone is afraid sometimes," Natalie said. "But if you talk to Jesus, he will help you be brave. His angels are watching over us."

The wind rattled around the coach house door.

Natalie thought it sounded nice, like Grandmother Wander's laughter.